Notes from the Domestic Underground

Someone gave me a mug during my first pregnancy. It says "Motherhood—It's not for wimps."

Amen

NOTES FROM THE DOMESTIC UNDERGROUND

www.carol-frey.com

Thanks go out to....

- the Beehive Queen, who brought this idea forth from a sea of emails,

- my friend John A. Stewart and the Amity Art Foundation, who provided energy and advice along with the belief that art of all types makes the world a better place,

- all the friends who encouraged me, including the girlfriend who read the first draft instead of watching Superbowl commercials (thanks!) and the one who pushed to make sure this made it to completion (thanks!)

- the many people who inspired these fictional stories. (If you think you recognize yourself, and are offended, then it wasn't you. Really.)

- and especially to my husband, sons, parents, extended family and friends who shared the many real-life adventures of the Domestic Underground!

Contents

Introduction to Notes from The Domestic Underground

The world is, indeed, a dangerous place. Hearts get broken. Entire governments tumble. The Atom Bomb lurks. The lintcatcher in the dryer catches on fire. A toilet explodes.

Carol Frey knows this world from down in the trenches, from the realest places there are: the kitchen floor with a filthy rag in her hand, the dinner table across from a glaring husband, the car full of screaming kids. It's perilous territory, this "domestic underground," and those trailblazers who've come before "Mama Bear" (Frey's nom-de-plume and alter ego) are no lot of shrinking violets—Erma Bombeck (whose *The Grass is Always Greener Over the Septic Tank* is the genre's bible), "Domestic Goddess" Roseanne Barr, Anne Taintor and her brilliant housewives-from-hell postcards, Phyllis Diller...the list goes on. Badass women all, they've been there, and lived to tell the dirty tale—laughing to keep from crying.

There's truth in every page here--and wit, and intelligence, and a big dose of common sense. Frey's "Mama Bear" has the kind of cherished perspective—truth-telling yet subtly sophisticated—that makes the world seem right, and places the really important things—family, friends, shoes, and cats—on the pedestals they deserve.

Christine Ohlman,
The Beneficent Beehive Queen
Singer/Songwriter

ON MOTHERHOOD: THE EARLY YEARS

Six Kids After All

I like kids. I wanted six, but my husband Rex wanted two. Since children are a cooperative effort, we have two. So I showed him. It took years of scheming. At first I thought I'd substitute cats, but more than three cats and my eyes itch and the house smells a little funny. Rex was even less cooperative about getting dogs than about having six kids.

So I used our two boys as bait.

I started out inviting kids to stay over with the boys. When our sons were small, any old children were fine for a playdate. They were pretty indiscriminate. If a couple that we knew "BC" ("Before Children") wanted time alone together, I'd volunteer. It was like a party. And I got another child.

Like the witch luring Hansel and Gretel to her home with sweets, I developed specialties:

chocolate cupcakes baked in ice cream cones from a recipe off the flour bag (and given an exotic name), macaroni and cheese from a 40-year-old cookbook, apple cake that my grandmother learned to make from HER grandmother. All kid-tested and kid-approved. We had one small group that enjoyed an annual First Day of Summer Vacation ritual. I bought cans of shaving cream, one per child, and several bottles of food coloring, and put the kids outside with the patio furniture. In an hour, the furniture and children were covered with light brown foam. I hosed everything and everyone off and then passed out snacks on the (miraculously clean!) patio table. The kids wrapped themselves in big beach towels and munched on crackers and cheese and cookies and fruit. And I had a big family, if only temporarily.

I honed my Temporary Family Enlargement skills.

"Come over," I'd say. "We'll have a party. I'll make cupcake cones/macaroni and cheese/apple cake." I lured them with old sheets to make tents with the sofa, and hot cocoa served in delicate china cups after lively games of "fox and geese" in freshly fallen snow. I gave every snack a fancy name and made up legends about the hot cocoa recipe because it was from scratch and tasted strange to the Instant Cocoa Generation.

I knew my plan was bearing fruit when an eight year old with an angel face asked shyly if I could be her godmother. She'd discussed it with her mother, as she'd lost her original godmother and they'd decided I could be a replacement.

Score.

Three kids. Our two boys and now Angel Face.

Then, another young teenager decided I'd be a

cool godmother. That was because I lent her books, and then discussed them with her. She learned to appreciate Saki and Orson Scott Card, thanks to me. And Dave Barry selections. Her parents are good friends with Rex and me. They didn't mind.

Four.

The reader's sister expressed envy. She likes to read, too. So there was the lure of the library as well as a shared passion for tea and chocolate. She pointed out that, since I was her sister's godmother, I'm really hers, too. I let it slip in conversation with her parents weeks later and found out she didn't even bother to tell them. She's quite an independent one. They didn't mind—either her recruiting a godmother or her attitude. Which is probably how she got to be so independent.

Five.

And then, of course, the Adorable Teenaged Hulk who stayed with us for some weeks while his divorced mother was on an extended training trip. Friends with both our boys, the Adorable Teenaged Hulk fell right into treating Rex and me as substitute parents. We fed him macaroni and cheese and nagged him about finishing his homework. He stumbled around with my two sons every morning, scratching himself and grunting along with them. Fit right in.

Six. Ah, success!

And now the Adorable Teenaged Hulk fixes our computer, Reader Number One organizes our eclectic home library and lends me Janet Evanovich books, and Reader Number Two supplies me with Russian chocolate. My original godchild, Angel Face, brings me to dance recitals and picnics.

But Rex was right, too. By borrowing the extra

kids, we don't have to put them through college.

Mama Bear sez: There are lots of people to befriend, and they don't have to be biologically connected.
Also, there's often a way around restrictions imposed by a husband.

Baby's First Word

Just the other day, a mom was obsessing about when her toddler was going to start talking. Or, rather, start speaking understandably in his mother's language – the child babbled incessantly, but not comprehensibly. I tried to calm her monthly-parenting-magazine-induced case of nerves. Children learn to talk when they are good and ready, and by the time they're in their mid-teens, they are almost all fully capable of communicating their innermost thoughts as well as all the stupid half-baked ideas they decide to use to torment their parents.

I calmed this mother by reminiscing about my older son, Bing. A big boy, when he was 18 months old other parents thought he was two or even older. One day, in the pediatrician's waiting room, Bing and I were playing with a plastic fantasy horse (smells like ice cream, fake jewels stuck on its butt and hair like a Disney Princess – obviously a "girl toy" but I'm cool).

The previous patient was leaving the examining room, and we heard a cheerful command ringing through the hallway.

"Say 'Bye-bye' to the doctor, Emmy!" sang out Emmy's well-groomed and apparently heavily-caffeinated Mom.

"Bye-bye," responded Emmy, cheerfully.

"Say 'Bye-bye, Doctor'," corrected Emmy's Mom, still cheerful in that well-caffeinated way.

"Bye-bye, Doctor," parroted Emmy, much less cheerfully.

The little family emerged into the waiting area, Emmy the Little Automaton still waving mechanically.

Emmy's Dad was along, too, smiling and silent. Emmy's Mom spotted Bing, who was watching the parade with what appeared to be horrified fascination, the toy pony still dangling forgotten from his hand.

She pounced on the innocent lad and started addressing him. "What a pretty horsie! Can you say 'pretty horsie'? Can you say 'pretty'? Say 'pretty'!" she cooed.

The first fruit of my loins stared at her in blatant disbelief.

"Say 'pretty'!" she demanded. "Can't you say 'pretty'?"

A dangerous expression shadowed Bing's cherubic features. He grasped the plastic toy in what could only be described as a threatening manner.

"Pret-ty. Say 'pret-ty hor-sie'!" A shrill note of rising hysteria crept into her voice.

I wasn't sure who I was saving. Emmy, all

ringlets and flounced dress and patent leather shoes, was still waving automatically at anything in her path. Emmy's Dad was still smiling, rather vacantly. Emmy's Mom was turning red. Bing was glowering. I put a gentling hand on Bing's back and smiled at Emmy's Mom.

"He doesn't speak on command," I explained softly.

She looked at me, flinched, then gathered her remaining dignity and her little family around her and fled the waiting room. Bing relaxed, flashed me a grateful look and turned his attention back to the toys.

I hoped that little Emmy would not grow up mutilating Barbie dolls. And I hoped that Bing would remember, when he was a teen-ager, that at least once his mother really understood him.

Baby's First Exclamatory Sentence

Many years ago I became a Stay At Home Mom with the birth of our first child, Bing. When Bing was about a year and a half old and I began to emerge from the fog of too little sleep, I decided to contribute more to the family, to make the nest more livable – in short, to wallpaper the bathroom.

The existing wallpaper was brown, with flowers and physically challenged butterflies. Definitely in need of a change. So I found a small, light colored and conservative print, sort of the anti-brown-with-butterflies pattern. Good Old Mom taught me how to wallpaper by doing all the difficult parts around the toilet and the sink. She left me two strips to paste on, just two straight shots to complete the room and glory in my accomplishment. I tacked them up while Bing, age one and one half, stacked blocks nearby. I admired my handiwork – and Mom's, of course, but she had returned home and I could pretend I'd done it all. It looked good, except the wall, without the flowers and butterflies, looked surprisingly empty. I remembered a gift I'd received last birthday, a hand-crafted decorative shelf sporting little gingerbread men and some early American detailing. Tucking Bing on my hip, I went in search of the stashed shelf.

I dug it out of the back of the extra bedroom closet and shook the dust off. Hmmm. The little gingerbread men were painted white with rather sinister-looking little painted-on faces. Not appropriate. Kind of creepy.

"Oh, s**t," I said.

Bing (of course!) perked up. He hadn't yet talked much, and definitely not enthusiastically. "Oh, thit!" he said, beaming.

"No, Sweetie, that's a Mommy word, just for Mommy to say."

"Oh, thit!" he responded, gleeful.

"Shhh, let's say 'Pretty ghostie,' Sweetie. Look at the pretty ghostie!"

"Oh, thit," Bing crowed.

My husband Rex came home two hours later and Bing greeted him with "Oh, thit!"

I had some explaining to do.

Angels Among Us

When our younger son, PJ, was about 5 years old, he came to me to discuss a conversation he'd had with one of his young friends. Georgie had told PJ that ghosts are bad and cause trouble for people. Georgie was quite afraid of ghosts, and assured PJ that he should be, too. This idea troubled PJ.

"Georgie is wrong," I reassured PJ. He was glad to hear that, and perked up. If Mommy said Georgie is wrong, it must be so. (Remember, PJ was only 5 years old, a long way from being a teen-ager. He was still at the stage where his thought process ran to "Mommy can make cupcakes, therefore Mommy is all-powerful.")

"Ghosts are just people without bodies," I continued. "Some are bad, but most are good. Do you know any really bad people who try to hurt you?"

PJ thought carefully. "No," he answered. I congratulated myself. I'd cleverly checked to see if PJ had problems with anyone in his relatively protected circle of acquaintances, while handling an entirely unrelated issue. What a Mom!

"There, then." I was on a roll. "And angels are just people without bodies, too, aren't they?"

"Yes," said PJ, almost breathless with anticipation.

What insights Mom was offering!

"So angels and ghosts are the same thing! You don't have to be afraid of ghosts!" I was triumphant.

PJ beamed. "I can hardly wait to tell Georgie!"

Georgie developed a sudden terror of angels.

Georgie's mother, with an extensive collection of angel figurines in everything from porcelain to papier-mache', did not speak to me for quite some time.

Beep! Beep!

Mothers develop a sense about some things. Like lies, total fabrications and undeniable BS. I have two sons, several godchildren, a past checkered with tutoring teenagers in math and grammar and a volunteer position working with drug addicts. I have combat training in recognizing Bull S**t.

So, to warn miscreants that my Mom-Sense was picking up nonsense, I began to beep. I fondly refer to this warning system, based on the age of the budding BS artist, as my Mom's Built In Lie Detector, Early Warning Fib Finder, or BS Meter. "Beep! Beep!" I go, and anyone from Angel Face, my first goddaughter, to my latest recovering meth addict at the rehab center where I volunteer, looks sheepish and confesses immediately.

Beep! Beep!

Well, OK, they may confess immediately, or they may plead innocent long enough for me to catch them in an undeniable falsehood. Or not. But they often laugh and, especially the heavily tattooed meth addicts, soften up and decide I might be OK, after all. My father, who is an accomplished fabricator, just laughs and tries again.

Now my husband Rex is trying to hone his BS meter.

I insist that it doesn't work on me. I never exaggerate, prevaricate, or falsely indicate.

Beep! Beep!

The Godmother

My goddaughter Angel Face and her sister, The Princess, came roaring up to me in church the other day.

"You lied to us!" accused The Princess. Angel Face nodded emphatically.

My mind raced. I'd lied to them a lot. Did they discover that my whole grain pancakes really aren't from an old Native American brunch recipe? Did they find out that the hot chocolate I make is really from a different box than their mother uses, and not an old European family secret after all, just a homemade mix reconstituted in a china cup with a peppermint stick? There are plenty of – um – STORIES to catch me on.

The girls are teens now, wearing make-up and all-too-revealing clothes (why aren't bhurkas required for all girls until they're 30 years old?

If these two were mine, they'd be wearing chastity belts instead of low-rider jeans). They're not naïve little kids, like they were when their all-too-trusting parents left them with me for a week that may have tried their credulity more than my wits. Throughout the week, I told them a lot of stories. My boys, Bing and PJ, just roll their eyes at me and, from a very early age, learned to think for themselves. I like to think they learned a valuable skill from listening to me. Apparently Angel Face and The Princess have just discovered my bad habit of lying to little kids, six years late.

"You said that if we hit the button to cross the street a lot of times, the light would change faster!" stated Angel Face, who could now be re-named Very Resentful Face.

"Yeah!" added The Princess, with a similarly Very Resentful Face.

"Wow," I answered. "You just figured that

out?"

They nodded with slit eyes and pursed lips.

"I'm awesomer than I thought!" I answered.

It was obviously not the right reaction. Their eyes got smaller and their lips tighter. I continued anyway. What were they going to do to me? They obviously weren't packing guns. Their jeans were too tight.

"It took you this long to figure it out? It kept you busy so I didn't have to listen to you two complain about how long it took for the 'walk' light to turn on. You felt more in control, I didn't have to listen to whining. A totally brilliant move on my part."

They held their poses briefly. Then their faces started to twitch and they burst into giggles. They still bombarded me with accusations, but I was sure I was forgiven.

"Wait 'til you have children," I said. "And godchildren." Whew, I thought to myself. My hot chocolate recipe is safe.

Mama Bear sez: Tell your kids a few harmless (but easily discovered) untruths so they learn to think for themselves at an early age.

They'll certainly hear enough lies throughout their lives. And besides, it's kind of fun.

Mothers' Day Celebrations

Over the many years that I've been a daughter and then a mother, I've seen a lot of different ways to celebrate Mothers' Day.

My own mother has been the victim of many a breakfast in bed consisting of a bowl of soggy breakfast cereal with cold toast and orange juice (my brother and I couldn't make coffee). We brought it to her on a cookie sheet with flowers made out of tissues and pipe cleaners, which we made as a final touch after preparing breakfast (meaning: after pouring the milk on the cereal, ensuring it had plenty of time to soak into cold slop). Mom loathes breakfast cereal, even when it still crunches. We knew that, but we didn't know how to make eggs, which my father claimed required a magic touch that it had taken my mother years to perfect. He, of course, had taught her. He hadn't taught us, because we were too young to use the stove. So Mom got very soggy cereal to celebrate Her Special Day.

She never complained. Dad snuck out of bed and did yard work before the ceremonial Breakfast in Bed was served.

Years later, my own children gave me breakfast in bed. Same menu.

I never complained, either. But my husband got out of bed early, for yard work. There must be a Fathers' Survival Guide that I don't know about.

One year, when the entire family (my husband, two young sons and me) went to the mall because the mall was air-conditioned and our house wasn't and it was a particularly summery Mothers' Day, I witnessed the perfect celebration. A young father herded three lively boys who dashed between stores and displays. He gathered them together in front of the same cookie kiosk we were patronizing.

Because I was already practicing to embarrass my children as soon as they were old enough to notice, I just had to talk to the busy dad. My children were still young enough to be more interested in the cookies on display than in how much I was humiliating them.

"You look busy," I commented

"Yes," he answered. "It's my wife's Mothers' Day present. She's at home, alone."

Lucky woman. Smart man.

And a happy Mothers' Day!

ON MOTHERHOOD: THEY'RE BIG AND HAIRY NOW

But You're a Mom!

My younger son, PJ, and I were observing our Traditional Rite of the Sixteenth Birthday and standing in line at the Department of Motor Vehicles to get him a learner's permit at the earliest possible moment. We stood in line for a long time. After an hour and fifteen minutes, I decided to comment on the mother and son combo standing in line ahead of us. I'd been admiring the mother for about forty-five minutes. She stood tall and lean, a Motorcycle Momma in skinny legged jeans, high boots, a camisole top and a gauzy shirt hanging open. She had a deep tan and streaked blond hair piled on top of her head, framing a well-made up, albeit mature-enough-to-be-his-mom face. I was impressed. (Understand, I'm a dumpy, over forty year old mom who wears flat sandals and baggy jeans and, sometimes, mascara and a de-frizzing hair product.) The gawky pre-pubescent standing next to this Vision of

Impossible Motherhood was not so impressive, but I figured he was a late bloomer. There was a family resemblance, so I figured he'd grow into a "James Dean: Rebel Without a Cause" look by the time he was 22.

I was polite. I whispered quietly to my son so I wouldn't make them uncomfortable.

"I wish I could look jazzy," I said.

"Huh?" he answered. (Age: 16 years old.)

"I wish I could look like her," I said, very quietly, and nodded toward them.

"Why?" PJ burst out, somewhat incredulous and not very quietly.

"Because she looks really good," I whispered.

"You CAN'T 'look really good,' Mom." PJ almost wailed.

"And why not?" I whispered louder, my eyes starting to glow red.

"Because you're a MOM," he answered, like I had the IQ of a pigeon, a turnip, or a human maternal unit.

Thanks, kid. Thanks a lot. But at least it takes the pressure off.

Too Stupid For Words

Any parent knows that there's a point in a child's life when he's amazed that his parents can breathe on their own, without life support. They are Too Stupid for Words. Sometimes, the child will even attempt to enlighten his parents on their inadequacies. So it was with Bing...

When Bing had an internet friend, "Summer," who sent him a photo, via e-mail, of a young woman in extremely brief shorts, sporting a lot of hair and a lot of curves, I suggested that he was being scammed by a 40+ year old pervert (who I dubbed "Bubba"). I was immediately labeled Too Stupid for Words and Probably Evil, Too. I obviously did not want my thirteen and a half year old son to find romantic bliss. Bing was Romeo to Summer's Juliet, and I was every evil Capulet and Montague rolled into one.

Unfortunately for me, I just couldn't keep quiet. Bing had to prove to me that he was a mature man of the world, hooking up with improbably curvaceous thirteen and a half year old girls via the miracle of the internet. I left him no choice. He found that Summer lived (imagine the coincidence!) near where the family would be vacationing in a month. He made elaborate plans to meet with her on the beach, and I offered that she would be welcome to dinner as soon as I was informed of the planned meeting. Although he didn't say it out loud, I could almost hear his voice saying "See, Mom, she's real. You, however, are Too Stupid for Words."

We went on vacation. The fateful day of the scheduled meeting arrived. Bing went to the beach, thankfully public and well-populated. He returned, much later, long past the time of meeting. He had a sunburn and a scowl, but no Summer on his arm. He was very quiet. I did not ask him about Summer, or about any older, creepy men who may have been lurking on the beach watching him.

I didn't hear any more about Summer after that, although I had ample more opportunities to prove myself stupid until Bing reached about age twenty and sometimes called me for advice, mostly about cooking and laundry.

Now, Bing is teaching me to use complicated computer things, like the internet. He just explained how to check for security on a web site, so I can safely shop on-line. Not only does he understand this stuff, but he can explain it to me so that it makes sense.

Now, he IS smarter than I am...and, regarding many points of modern technology, I may be, well, ALMOST Too Stupid for Words...

Mama Bear sez: Parents get smarter as their children age. At least in some areas.

Mom Skills: Tender Moments in the Car

Driving leads to deep, meaningful conversations. An intimacy develops when we're engulfed in a metal cocoon with another person, sequestered from the outside world (unless the cell phone rings, the radio is on or there's a lot of traffic...).

So time in the car with Son Number Two, PJ, is a valued thing. Sometimes, PJ uses it to ask me deep questions. He once asked me about how someone learns how to be a parent. (Once I'd realized that this question did not mean I was about to be a grandmother and returned the car to the road after I'd swerved onto the shoulder, I told him "trial and error." And I started breathing again.)

This day, PJ cleared his throat and then hesitated.

"Mom, can I ask you a question?"

"Of course, Son," I answered.

"It's a little bit weird," he continued.

"OK." Yes! A chance to flex my Mom Skills Muscles.

"It's a little bit embarrassing," he added.

"Go on," I encouraged, almost breathless with anticipation. I was going to shine as a Modern Understanding Mom. Unless he was going to ask me how to tell his father we were about to be grandparents. Then I wasn't going to shine so much.

"Um..." He paused again. I let the silence deepen and practiced a concerned, interested look while continuing to keep my eyes on the road. After all, I was driving. And getting a little worried.

"Why does eating asparagus make your pee smell funny?" he finally blurted out.

Rats. I don't know.

"Phytochemicals. Yep, phytochemicals in the vegetable matter," I answered with what I hoped was a knowledgeable intonation that wouldn't allow further questions.

"It's OK, Mom, I didn't think you'd know, either. I'll look it up on the internet when we get home," he assured me. "And then I'll tell you."

Busted.

Chaperone to the X-Men

Son Number Two, PJ, asked if my husband Rex or I would help chaperone a school event. It's a fundraiser for cancer research. The high school students form teams, turn the sports fields into a suburban version of a third world refugee camp with tents and Port-a-Potties, and spend all night taking turns walking around the track to somehow magically turn pledges into donations.

They need adult chaperones.

I'm a good mom and wife, so I agreed to do this. PJ signed me up for the midnight-to-3AM shift because that slot was hard to fill. He promised there would be snacks, so I didn't protest too much. Then he explained that their team had a slogan, "X-terminate Cancer," and they'd have t-shirts with the slogan on it. Each person's shirt would have the name of one of the "X-Men" characters on it. Big and muscular, he was going to be "Colossus."

I said if I was going to be a chaperone, I wanted to be Professor Xavier.

He said no.

I said that if I was doing the midnight-to-3AM shift, I should get to be Professor Xavier.

He still said no, but reminded me there'd be lots of snacks.

I told him that if I didn't get to be Professor Xavier, I'd bring a big flashlight along and sit outside their tent in a lawn chair and periodically leap up, shine the flashlight into the tent and holler "This is the chaperone! Are there any unwanted pregnancies being started in there?"

He said I wasn't going to be the only

chaperone, that each team was going to have two adults there at all times. The other chaperone would help chaperone me.

I said I still wanted to be Professor Xavier, and I resented having another chaperone, which shows a distinct lack of trust on the part of the school administration.

He said he wished he'd convinced his father to volunteer instead of me. Rex just laughed, and didn't offer to take my place.

I'm counting on good snacks.

And I'm bringing a big flashlight.

Parenting and Dictionaries

I've been getting a crash-course in "Helicopter Parenting," which appears to mean hovering over your children until it drives them crazy. I don't understand it much – probably because of how I was raised.

We learn parenting skills from our parents. That may be why it looks like insanity runs in families. It does, but it's learned, not genetic.

Growing up, my father's mantra as he left home each morning to go to work was "Go to school and learn a lot, so you can support your dear old gray-haired mother and father in the style to which they would like to become accustomed." He said it like that, "in the style to which they would like..." He's a grammar nutcase. He owns the complete collected short stories of Ernest Hemingway and of Mark Twain. He tried to tell me I couldn't understand these authors, so I shouldn't bother trying to read them (you can guess what THAT did—I cracked those books open whenever my parents weren't around to catch me).

If I didn't know what a word meant, in reading or conversation, Dad would tell me to look it up in the dictionary. For a major Christmas present the year I was ten years old, he and Mom collaborated on purchasing a giant, twenty-pound, "Complete and Unabridged and Pretty Darn Heavy Random House Dictionary With Which to Torment Your Children."

My best friend Becky fabricated a game. She was fascinated by the dictionary (probably because it wasn't HER Christmas present). She started looking up dirty words it in. She discovered that you could form a chain of words – look up one word, preferably something quite innocent, like "ox," and then look up words from the definition of ever-increasing naughtiness until you couldn't find a new one to look up and were dead-ended.   The longest chain wins. She'd grab "ox" and I'd pick "stamen" and off we'd go.   We both grew well-informed on scientific names for vulgar expressions.

Now my father pretends he doesn't remember giving my brother and me a dictionary for Christmas. So I don't feel obligated to tell him about the game Becky and I used to play.   And I gave my kids each a pretty hefty dictionary for their birthdays.

Hey, at least they each have their own.   And they weren't their MAIN birthday presents. And they may learn the medically correct names for body parts.

Mama Bear sez: Let 'em learn all they can, even if it's medically correct terms for dirty words. Doctors use 'em.

Homework

PJ's art project finally emerged from one of the myriad backpacks that he'd been toting throughout the school year. It's a strange pyramid-shaped clay sculpture with an unrealistic collection of eyes, noses and mouths.

I remember that assignment. During one of our bonding moments in the minivan on the way to soccer practice, PJ had described the assignment to me. I was driving because he was still putting on his shoes. PJ casually started the conversation.

"I have an art project to do. It's kind of weird. Maybe you can help," he said. And then the killer line: "You're good with this type of thing because you're real creative, so I thought you might have an idea."

My mind reeled. That sounded like a

compliment. From my teenager. I tried to concentrate but PJ's first sentence ricocheted through my mind like a pre-schooler on a jelly bean binge.

The art teacher had picked a theme – out of the air, it appeared, because I didn't understand it at all. The theme involved integrating two totally unrelated items into a working whole. Sounds like teenage life to me.

Seriously, PJ and his teammates have cut their hair into matching punk styles, shaved their heads, and are now contemplating giving up shaving for the duration of the fall sports season to show solidarity for their soccer team. They're experts at combining unrelated things and imagining a connection. I'm glad they aren't promoting tattoos and piercings as a way to better understand British Literature class. One of them could undoubtedly find a relationship there somewhere – and convince his classmates, and they'd all end up with a picture of Jane Austen permanently inked onto an arm or calf – or worse.

Maybe I just didn't understand very well. I was driving. The traffic was heavy. I was distracted by the compliment.

I suggested three projects, trying to open a discussion of the artistic merits of various juxtapositions. Mother/son quality time in the car.

PJ sent me a withering look.

"Those are bad ideas," he said.

I try not to let criticism get to me. Especially if it's criticism of how well I do someone else's homework.

I sent him a withering look. Much more withering than his look, but hampered by its limited duration. He probably would have wilted into the seat if I hadn't been driving and had to make it more of a withering quick glance because of the traffic.

"It's not MY homework," I answered.

Gotcha.

Momma Bear sez: It's not my homework, so don't expect me to do it. I've already finished high school.

PJ the Hooligan

At the tender age of seventeen and a new Senior in High School, PJ started showing school spirit outside of his own personal soccer field. He began attending girls' soccer games. And boys' football games (guess what, girls attend those games – big draw).

One day, in the testosterone-fueled blindness of youth, he donned his t-shirt that stated boldly "Hooligan" in big red letters, a pair of baggy jeans ("It's the fashion, Mom!") with two inches of his underwear showing at the top ("It's the fashion, Mom!") and took his unshaven face ("It's the fashion, Mom!" "For movie stars, PJ, not teenagers who look like they're growing mold instead of a beard." "Mom, really, it's cool. And anyway, my ride's here already, I don't have time to shave.") to a football game. Where there were girls, Bad Influences, and a cop-on-overtime.

Uh-oh.

PJ is not a small child. He's six feet tall in stocking feet and close to 200 pounds of muscle. He plays soccer and lacrosse, and the coaches mostly use him to prevent players from the other team from getting into scoring position. The football coach stalked him for two years, drooling over PJ's sheer bulk. So when my baby, unshaven and large, wears a shirt proclaiming he is a hooligan, he is quite believable.

At the football game, Mr. Popular Jerk (note the initials, yes, I'm referring to my very own PJ, fruit of my loins and darling of my heart) accepted a drink from a soda bottle from another kid. He took one sip, then another. He acted stupid, drawing the attention of Cop-on-Overtime.

I'm at home, minding my own business and

watching an old movie, a genuine chick flick (which doesn't happen often, living with three testosterone-soaked males). The phone rings. It's PJ, sounding nervous.

"Mom? Can you come and pick me up at the football game? There's a problem. Don't tell Dad."

Words to chill.

"What's wrong?" I'm not even hysterical yet because I'm such a cool Mom. "Are you bleeding?"

"No."

"Is anyone else bleeding?"

"No."

"Dead?"

"No."

"What is it?"

"Uh...there's this cop here who wants me to call you. He thinks I've been drinking...'"

Silly cop. PJ's on the varsity team. He doesn't drink, it's forbidden, and illegal...uh-oh.

"I'll be right there," I said.

PJ and Cop-On-Overtime are outside the football game gate. Cop-On-Overtime and PJ appear to be chatting cheerfully until Paul looks up and becomes agitated. He is not happy to see I've brought Rex. What did he think? That I wouldn't bring back-up?

"What's going on?" I ask, miles short of panic. There's no blood, no bodies.

"Um..." PJ began, and several minutes later I

come to understand that he is trying NOT to tell Rex and me that he was drinking some vile alcoholic mix from a soda bottle.

Cop-On-Overtime is concerned about my reaction. He does not, however, pull his gun out, or even his tazer. He tries to convince me that PJ is a good child and he even offered to let him back into the football game.

"Not a chance! He's grounded for two weeks and I'm taking away his driver's license! He's coming home right now, with his father and me, and we are going to let him explain everything to his friends!" I continue to spew threats like devil-possessed pea-soup vomit, until Cop-On-Overtime backs off, wishes PJ luck, and dives for cover. Rex takes my arm. PJ is afraid of me. I think my head is spinning around and my eyes are glowing red.

"Mom. I thought Dad would be more pissed than you'd be," PJ says, awestruck with fear.

I stupidly call my parents for help, proof that demonic possession interferes with judgement. Big fat help my father is. He's over 75, with a ponytail and tattoos and a motorcycle (at least it's not a Hog with naked women painted on it, small consolation). He rushes over, on the motorcycle. We call PJ into the family room, where my father and he share the couch. PJ looks wary, but the wariness seems to be mostly directed at me.

"I'm disappointed in you, PJ. Seriously disappointed. I thought I'd been a better influence on you. Really, I'm worried about you." My father looks at PJ with eyes filled with sorrow.

PJ just looks back. He knows my father (apparently better than I do) and is waiting for the punch line. It comes.

"Rum and Dr. Pepper! How abominable! Beer,

or bourbon, OK.   But rum and Dr. Pepper! You've got to have better taste than that." Dad still looks sorrowful.   Rex laughs at my father. PJ laughs at his grandfather.

My head is rotating again and my eyes are glowing red.   I really wish I could send my father to his room and ground him for two weeks.

Auntie Potty Mouth

My parents host an annual family reunion vacation at a rented beach house. From 10 to 18 family members gather in a big beach house and try not to fight too much. It builds character along with tans.

My 16 year old niece Elle, tall and leggy and hormonally overwhelmed, lost every shred of self control in a crowded restaurant about mid-week, courtesy of a few well-placed comments whispered by her older brother. It happens. He was delighted, she was humiliated.

"I lost it. I was mad and I got loud. I dropped the f-bomb," she confessed to me.

"That's bad," I said. I sounded unsympathetic. She looked surprised.

"It was," she agreed, sounding confused. She'd

obviously expected me to agree that her brother is annoying beyond endurance, or to otherwise absolve her of her outburst.

"Yep," I said. "You're not qualified to swear."

"Huh?" She was no longer thinking about how stupid she was. Now she was thinking about how stupid I was. It was an improvement for a hormonally overwhelmed teenager.

"Yes," I explained. "See these thighs?" I pointed to just above my knees. I was wearing shorts.

She nodded.

"Crepe-y."

"What's that?"

"See these little wrinkles everywhere? Your thighs are silky, mine are like crepe. Like crepe paper, or crepe fabric, with little wrinkles all over."

She nodded, impressed. I sort of wished she hadn't understood quite so readily.

"Silky thighs," I said, pointing to her legs, bracketed by extremely short cutoffs and decorative sandals. "Crepe-y thighs," I continued, pointing to the slivers of thigh peeking out from below my linen walking shorts.

She nodded again.

"When you have crepe-y thighs, your compensation is that you can say anything you want, including swearing like a sailor who lost his rum ration. As long as you have silky thighs, you simply do not have the right to swear. It is a privilege that comes with crepe-y thighs."

She nodded again.

The next day, under barbs from her brother, I overheard Elle muttering to herself.

"Crepe-y thighs, silky thighs.   Crepe-y thighs, silky thighs."

At least we had no more teenaged meltdowns in public places.

And I switched to wearing Capri pants.

Helicopter Mom Decommissioning Program

Rex and I went to PJ's college orientation. It looked like two days of vacation, and maybe they'd feed us well and we could bond with PJ one last time before he headed off for the wide world of University in Major Metropolitan Area (we'll refer to it as "Almost-Gotham U.").

No such luck. He asked us not to go. He even tried to convince us that parents weren't supposed to go, or at least weren't encouraged to go. He lied. We got a lot of mailings urging us to attend. And we did, in spite of PJ's wishes.

PJ disappeared with a couple of friends and acquaintances and newly found Best Friends (yay for social media) within minutes of our arrival on campus. So Rex and I resolved to enjoy our two days in The Major Metropolitan

Area.

Instead, we went to some of the orientation talks, notably "Holding On and Letting Go," presented by the counseling department. The Woman In Charge asked for volunteer parents to form an impromptu panel to discuss the difficulties in letting a child actually leave home and go to college. Four parents were chosen, and took turns sniveling about their fears and sorrows and sufferings at the thought of their children being thrown into the rigors of megabucks-per-year Life Preparation at Almost-Gotham U.

One mom in designer Capri pants and a store-bought tan related how hard it was for her to let go of her daughter's hand when they crossed the metro-train tracks on the edge of the campus. She wanted desperately to hold the young woman back, she explained, but then realized something: her daughter is legally an adult! She drives a car! She is studying to be an engineer! At prestigious Almost-Gotham University! She would be crossing that street WITHOUT HER MOTHER hundreds of times over the next years! The other parents on the panel nod sagely, and Tom, the only man on the panel, begins his story.

It is sorrowful. His only son is leaving home to go to college. Life will never be the same. Tom's eyes well with tears. His voice cracks and unreleased sobs choke him (before I can). Tom is whining, and I'm afraid I'll start, too.

A woman sitting next to me, in jeans and a no-name (or at least "no little well-known embroidered hanging sheep or horse and rider") collared knit shirt turned to me. She was not sympathetic to Tom's plight.

"Get the roses and tiara, and award him the washing machine. He's won Queen for the Day for the saddest hard-luck story," she said to me and rolled her eyes. "There may still be coffee in the parents' lounge. I'm outta here." She stood up and walked out of the room while Tom was still sniveling.

Rex watched her go. He'd heard her remarks. Then Rex looked at Tom.

"Maybe there are muffins, too" said Rex.

We followed our new friend to the parents' lounge.

Mama Bear sez: Kids grow up. It beats them living in your basement drinking beer and playing video games all day.

Dismissed!

We moved PJ into his dorm. The university is very well-organized. Each student and set of parents received instructions via postcard, letter and e-mail. The parents were told the time slot they had for move-in: four hours scientifically selected for maximum efficiency and minimal confusion. The parking lot was assigned, with closing times named. "The lot closes at 11 PM" warns the postcard. "All cars remaining in the lot after it closes will be towed." This fit in with the warnings from the Head of Campus Security, a retired police chief with a friendly attitude who cheerfully related to parents (many aghast at the effrontery of the student in the story, totally missing the point the Head of Campus Security was trying to push) how one newly arrived freshman inquired about getting a restraining order on his mother because she wouldn't leave the campus after moving him into his room.

Burly men of various ages in matching t-shirts and matching muscles met us in our assigned parking lot. "Bouncers!?" I thought. But no, they were hired to help us unload our cars, vans, SUVs and moving trucks into carts (the type large hotels use for laundry) and push them around campus, up moving ramps strategically placed over granite stairways and across streets guarded by armies of police, student guides and more hired muscle. They'd pass the carts off to another team at street corners. "Ugh. Ullum," they'd grunt, which probably meant something, and the next team would push the carts up a ramp or across a street or around an obstacle.

We should have gotten another cart and climbed into it ourselves. These guys were way too fast for me, and much more efficient than Rex or PJ. We could've just been whisked along with PJ's jeans, binders and microwaveable popcorn in handy packets.

In no time (almost – really more like ½ hour), we were outside PJ's new room and unloading the cart. I made the bed (I'm still his mom!) and PJ moved his clothes into the nondescript bureau. This would be the last time his socks would ever see the inside of that drawer, if his room at home was any indicator of the future. He decided he needed a shower. I decided I needed an iced coffee. Rex decided he needed to get out of the dorm room. We agreed to meet at the Parents' Reception, conveniently held in a central location on campus.

When PJ caught up with us, he reported that his roommate had arrived. He'd walked into the room après shower, wearing a towel and a grin, and there they were. Per PJ, Roommate's Mom commented that PJ seemed to be comfortable in the dorm setting already.

PJ has been working out for months, and sports rather impressive guns/pythons/biceps. I think he was making sure that he got undisputed first pick of sides of the room.

We each had a stale bagel (any bagel over 5 hours old is stale, as any NY deli connoisseur will tell you) and a bottle of juice and went to the bookstore.   PJ casually commented that he'd run into some friends he'd made at Student Orientation over the summer.   They'd planned to watch the televised football game that afternoon, so we only had about 45 minutes.

"Just enough time," PJ explained, "to go to the bookstore and get books."

Several hundred dollars later, PJ hefted the big box o' knowledge that we'd just purchased and told us we had to hurry, he was late for the game.   We asked if he needed any help getting his internet connection checked or his College Dollars Card.   PJ assured us he could handle it, and repeated that the game had started and his friends were expecting him.

Rex and I had been dismissed.

We later found that the Student Orientation had included a lecture on 15 Ways to Get Your Parents Out of Your Hair, put on by upperclassmen.

They pretended it was a joke. I think it's the only presentation that PJ really paid attention to.

Mama Bear sez: Be grateful they're independent because, if you think about it, you really don't want them living with you forever. Eventually, you may want grandchildren.

Moving Out and Moving On

So the youngest one goes off to college. I've been upset, really upset, teeth-gnashing and bone-rattling upset, for two weeks about PJ leaving home. Even though I know better, and was prepared, and had vowed not to allow myself to get all upset, I got all upset. So I did what I always do when I'm upset and don't understand how to fix it. I called my mother.

I have a role model, you know.

She laughed at me.

"I understand, Pumpkin," she drawled. "When your little brother left home I went out back and knelt down and pounded on the ground and screamed." She paused. "Your father didn't understand." She got wistful-sounding and her drawl thickened. "I felt my usefulness was over."

Thanks, Mom, I hadn't been thinking THAT before. I'm going to go looking for a convenient ice floe to crawl onto and wait for the Great Beyond to catch up to me.

Mom continued. "I thought I could find meaning in my job. That's why I wanted to keep working."

She had been bossing around the U.S. office of a high-end importer of technical equipment in the nearby Big City, a long commute from their small fashionably country home town. She was hired to be the executive assistant to the director of the office. She ended up being the Lead Dictator. I thought she wanted to keep working so she could keep bossing people around once the kids had left. I didn't know she'd been looking for meaning. This could turn into a touching moment, shared confidences via telephone line. I could almost hear strains of violin music pulling tears from an audience.

Mom's voice crisped a bit into raspiness. She sounded like she was pulling on a cigarette, although she'd quit, "just for today," decades ago.

"Your father came out of the house after a few minutes. I'd worked myself up by then, and he probably thought the neighbors were going to call the police. He brought me a double bourbon, neat. I took a sip, stopped screaming and carrying on, then toddled back into the house after three sips, dutifully finished it and took a nap. When I woke up, I baked cookies and sent them to your brother, your cousin who was in the Navy and Little Lenny – he was in the half-way house at the time and they'd let him get packages there if he shared with the counselors. Oh, and I took some to the neighbors because they had just put their cat to sleep and taking over a casserole seemed like too much for a cat, even a Siamese with a pedigree. And the rest of the cookies I took to work and passed around after I sent out the memo with the new rules for the lunch room."

She'd found meaning, indeed.   Dictator and Cookie Baker.

It worked.   I didn't feel so wretched about PJ moving out.   I packed him extra sheets and towels, and sorted some socks he'd left behind, tucking them into corners of the box.

I baked cookies and packed some in with PJ's sheets and socks.   I ate some, too.

Mama Bear sez: Get advice from your mama, and follow it if it sounds good.

Graduation of Son Number One

Saturday night I sat with my husband Rex, surrounded by hundreds of parents and family members of other graduates of a small, private liberal arts college in Pennsylvania's heartland. We formed a group joined together in both worry about rain disrupting the outdoor Baccalaureate ceremony and confusion about the term "baccalaureate" (it just means a degree program at a college or, in the U.S., a sermon delivered before a graduation ceremony to a graduating class – I looked it up before I went to it so I'd know what I was getting into).

All the grandparents and the graduate's godmother and great-aunt had joined us. We'd wrapped them in blankets against the evening chill and damp, except for my mother, who was, as always, fully prepared and sported a fashionable rain coat layered over a heavy sweater. My father rides a motorcycle and would have to be under a greater threat than chilly drizzle on a manicured college campus to drape himself in an afghan in public. He rides a gentleman's bike, a BMW touring motorcycle with custom details, but there is still an image to uphold. And he has tattoos. No little blankets in public for him.

I'd organized the three groups to meet at the hotel and find their way to the Chinese restaurant for a celebration dinner (Son Number One likes Chinese), found and retrieved one of the groups (who'd gotten lost for twenty minutes on the ten minute trip to the restaurant), then gotten everyone returned to the campus and seated for the Baccalaureate ceremony (no one was happy with our seats, especially the man behind our group who was treated to Great-Aunt's plum-wine fueled giggle and explanation that the chair was cold on her butt – he solemnly thanked her for sharing). It started to drizzle, lightly. A young graduate droned on, somewhat pompously listing all the significant, news-worthy events she could remember from her young life (my class – so long ago – had listed Kent State and Vietnam, she concentrated on the War on Terror and school shootings).

I pulled up the hood on my raincoat as umbrellas popped up around me. The hood was deep. Alone at last! I'd also had a glass of plum wine at dinner...I began to doze off.

Graduation ceremonies send our children on to start their adult life. When Son Number One was little and NEVER SLEPT, I'd always promised myself naps when he was grown up. So I started. Right away.

Bing's New Car and the Puddles of Drool

Our older son, Bing, is now old enough – and financially set enough – for a car. He wanted a Honda Del Sol. He's ALWAYS wanted a Honda Del Sol, or at least since he was old enough to read car magazines (and for a man child in the U.S. of A. that would be – how old? – six?).

They don't make the Del Sol model anymore. It has only two seats. His younger brother says it's a sports car for little old ladies. How will we ever find a place to get it repaired? How will Bing ever find one?

Well, as a Mom Who Knows How to Worry, I decided that these were Bing's problems. He found several cars, in various states and in various states of customization (the one with the miniature disco ball, purple strobe lights under the chassis and the day-glo paint job gave me pause, especially when he gave it consideration).

We ended up driving through two states to pick up a conservative (ha!) black Del Sol with discreet (double "Ha!") red and black pinstripes. We drove home caravan-style, connected by cell phone and stopping to meet my parents for a late lunch on the way home.

I knew I was in trouble when my father (he of the tattoos and motorcycle trips) drooled over the car, got a ride in it and came back all starry-eyed. Then my mother (known to ride on the motorcycle as well, but tattoo-free – I think) complimented Bing on his excellent choice of vehicles, telling him what a fine investment he'd made (for heaven's sake, Mom, it's a two-seater! It's over 12 years old! They don't make them any more!). Then, my mother got a ride in it, came back drooling and with starry eyes. Meanwhile, my father explained to me what an excellent choice of vehicles it is, and what a fine investment. I smiled and nodded outwardly, and shuddered inwardly.

Then, after we returned home, Bing took ME for a ride. And his father. And his brother. Not all at once, of course. After all, it's a two-seater. But it's an excellent investment, and a fine vehicle.

Now there are three puddles of drool by where the Del Sol is parked. I offered to fill up the gas tank if he lets me take it to work tomorrow...

PJ: Engineer

PJ attends an urban college, and decided that the dormitory life was too insulated, too expensive, and, although he didn't say this to us, probably too confining. He moved into an aged townhouse-style apartment with four other engineering students, creating an outpost of testosterone and questionable taste in a "borderline" neighborhood convenient to their college. Narrow, enclosed stairs twist upwards to the second floor, where two bedrooms and a bathroom spread out in spacious and shabby splendor. Almost identical stairs wind to the almost identical third floor.

Newly purchased mattresses bend, and make it up those treacherous stairs.

Newly purchased box springs don't. Don't bend, and don't make it up those treacherous stairs.

Not even the full-sized box springs for a relatively modest double bed. None of the students own a monastic single bed, advertisement of chastity and invitation to mockery. One proudly shows his newly acquired bedroom set, a vast king-sized bed with a mirrored headboard and built-in bedside tables which appear to miraculously float on each side. A matching dresser continued the theme of curlicues and gilt that would make a Reno whorehouse's residents blush with the excess. He was proud, as only a 20 year old could be – at least a 20 year old who'd scored used furniture that would NEVER fit up the stairs but who doesn't care because he's got the first floor bedroom.

Over sandwiches at a nearby pub, the Fabulous Five discussed their box spring dilemma among themselves and, since we were paying for the sandwiches, with Rex and me.

"We'll figure it out," was the consensus among

the new renters. "After all, we're engineers!"

I didn't correct them. They're engineering students, and still pretty far from their diplomas.

Rex and I left Almost-Gotham City and drove home. We discussed the engineering possibilities that had been reviewed at dinner. One wanted to saw the box springs in pieces and then figure out putting them back together after all the pieces were upstairs. Luckily, he didn't have a saw. Another planned an elaborate system of hinges. Another thought the box springs should be carefully dismantled and re-built.

The next day, about noon, I got a phone call from PJ.

"Mom?" he said. "Do you have any ideas on how to get the box springs up the stairs?"

I carefully kept the grin out of my voice, if not

off my face. "Call the landlord. This has happened before. Also, call the mattress store. They've run into this, too, I'm sure." I was also pretty sure I sounded thoughtful and concerned, with no hint of glee traveling down the phone lines.

"Do you have the number for the mattress store?"

SCORE: Mom: 1, Engineering students: 0

(The mattress store had a two-part box spring for a full-size mattress, which they delivered and exchanged, and all are happy. Especially Mom.)

Mama Bear sez: When you score big, try not to gloat. Too much. Or too publicly.

When Cute Ends –And a Theory on Why

I met Andrea for coffee. She'd called me and sent the middle-aged woman's version of the "Bat Signal." Instead of a spotlight with a silhouette of a flying mammal, she used the telephone and wailed about her teenaged daughter, Brittany. It was definitely an emergency.

We met in the local coffee shop fifteen minutes later. Batman has a "Bat-a-rang" on his high-tech utility belt, and travels to the emergency via Batmobile. We middle-aged women use caffeine and donuts and travel via minivan. I had the caffeine at home, but no sugar-confetti-covered confections. Hence, the Donut Palace, and a corner table in the back.

Andrea nervously arranged her two pink-frosted donuts on a napkin and then stirred Splenda into her double-mocha latte. Go figure. I didn't use sugar, or pretend sugar. I got my ration from the Boston cream oozing pudding onto my napkin.

"Brittany used to be so sweet," Andrea told me. "And so cute. And so loving."

"Yep," I answered. "And she'll be moving out in a year, right?"

"Yes," Andrea began to sob. I handed her some tissues from my purse (even with the kids out of the house, I remain an ever-vigilant mom, carrying tissues and a wholesome snack almost wherever I go). She told me about shopping with her daughter, and how now the girl hates everything her mother likes, wears torn jeans and too much eye make-up in unflattering shades and colors purple streaks in her bleached hair.

"Mm-hm," I nod. I had a mouth full of Boston

cream.

"She was always my baby!" sobbed Andrea.

"Mm-hm." I had another mouthful of Boston cream. I figured Andrea would be ready for my wisdom after she'd had a donut and about a third of her double-mocha latte.

Between sobs, Andrea nibbled on a pink donut. She sipped her latte. Her sobs quieted.

"You're such a good friend," she said, a sob catching her voice and adding a slight hitch.

"Mm-hm," I answered. More Boston cream.

"What can I do?" Andrea's tear-streaked eyes peered over the top of her cup. One donut down, and she was well into the latte. Ready for my advice.

"Brittany was an adorable toddler," I said.

Andrea nodded and tears welled up in her eyes.

"If she was still as cute as she was then, you'd never be able to let her go. And if she didn't think you were stupid and boring, she'd never be able to move out. It would be too hard."

By the time we finished our caffeine and sugar, we agreed that Brittany had been adorable and would be, again, but for now she had to be horrible so that everyone could bear to lose her to college, and she could bear to leave. It was self-protection.

My work, and the donuts, were finished.

Parenting Education

It was my father's birthday. I got reflective. Probably some lingering hormonal problem related to incipient menopause.

I called him after his motorcycle ride but before his lunch engagement (which included wearing a paper crown at a fast food restaurant – no, my father is NOT suffering from dementia, just taking advantage of having gray hair and indulging his childish habit of shocking people – and also my mother is a saint, or maybe just likes the entertainment). We reminisced a bit. PJ, my younger son, recently asked how someone learns to be a parent. I learned from my parents: My father taking me for my first motorcycle ride, at age 3. My father and mother getting me pony riding lessons, at age 4, from squinty-eyed Farmer Norton, who fast became my hero (he had ponies). My father calling me his "Big Buddy" at age 4 and teaching me how to skim the foam off the beer brewing in the basement before taxation closed down Dad's Home Brewery (I still use one of the crocks as an end table). Dad teaching me how to open beer bottles and bring them to him, age 5. Days of maternally-sanctioned hooky from elementary and high school. Dad teaching me to drive on a manual transmission the first couple of lessons, so when he let me try an automatic, it seemed easy.

And a memory that has stayed vivid for 30+ years: Dad at dinner time with my visiting Hawaiian roommate, a porcelain beauty of Japanese extraction whose silence gave evidence of her discomfort. Mom asked her what she thought of the current dinner topic, and Dad spoke up: "Don't bother Robin. She's Oriental, and they're all inscrutable." I sank into my chair. Mom rolled her eyes. Robin smiled shyly at my father. For the rest of her four years at college, Robin periodically explained to people who expected dramatics from her – or even a strongly worded opinion – that she was inscrutable. She used it to justify her rather fabulous ability at all manner of card games. She even used it in her description for the senior yearbook. Finally, at our college graduation, a dry-eyed Robin watched as the other members of our group hung onto each other weeping. She patted everyone who tried to cling damply to her, but remained serene in the face of all the emoting.

Until she saw my father. She ran to him (surprisingly fleet for a young lady in a pair of strappy high-heeled sandals) and flung herself into his arms. "Oh Mr. Frey," she sobbed, "I'm going to miss you SO much!" My father was as flattered as he was bemused. He uncertainly patted Robin's back as she clung to him, head buried in his chest and arms clutching his sides. She was inconsolable for the rest of the festivities. Dad had a damp patch on his shirt that lasted the rest of the afternoon. Mom invited Robin to visit anytime and, if she was inclined to leave her Hawaiian paradise home, to live with them while job hunting – or working – on the mainland.

So that's how I learned to be a parent. An eclectic education, indeed. My kids, so far, have survived.

ON
HOUSEKEEPING

Silver Linings and Opportunities

Lightning. Thunder. Rain. Power outage. Sump pump. Uh-oh.

At 5:00 AM per our battery-backed up alarm clock, my husband Rex slipped out of bed to prepare for a manly outing with one of our sons, PJ. I ignored him. It was easy.

At 5:03 AM, Rex came back into our room.

"There's four inches of water in the basement," he announced.   Like he expected me to do something.

I cracked open an eye. He wasn't going to let me ignore this. He waited, expecting action from me.

"Why?" I croaked.   I was buying time

underneath the warm covers.

"It's raining and the sump pump is off because the electricity is off." Tones of doom. The manly outing was going to be put off, and I was going to have to get wet feet.

I got up. I pulled on an extremely ratty sweatsuit and rain boots and went to inspect. Sure enough, ping pong balls, a floating kitty litter pan and assorted unidentified debris bobbed merrily in four inches of cold water. Rex hadn't exaggerated.

Toby the Wonder Cat stared longingly at the kitty litter pan from the safety of the third basement step. He looked uncomfortable. First things first, I thought, and waded in to rescue the cat's floating comfort facility and relocate it to higher ground.

Two hours and one rented generator later, the waters were receding and we were emptying the basement of ruined leftover wallpaper and old boxed magazines. Rex and PJ worked grimly. They saw devastation. I saw opportunity as I hauled a box of wet National Geographic magazines to the garage.

"Quick," I hissed to PJ while Rex was occupied with checking the generator. "Get the two boxes of ski magazines from the guest room closet and bring them down here for a good soaking."

Rex had been keeping them since the late 70's, along with the National Geographic magazines (does anyone, ever, throw these out?). Too bad about that flood. All those magazines, a total loss. Every last one of them.

I hope PJ doesn't rat me out. I think he wants a car now.

Mama Bear sez: Every cloud has a silver lining. Find it and take advantage of it.

Housekeeping Help: Will Use Spiders

One fine day, with the prospect of family visits looming on the horizon, I tackled the housecleaning.

I'm NOT a clean freak. I'm not even a neat freak. If I can find things and there aren't any unexpected – and visible – life forms, I'm good with that. Once, living in a house tucked among trees and bugs, I kept a spider in the bathroom behind the toilet. She kept the bugs down, and I only had to remove the dried bug shells from under her web. I knew it was a "her" because she finally produced several egg casings. Days before the casings erupted with hundreds of tiny spiderlings, I relocated the entire family – mother and all the progeny-to-be – to the great outdoors.

So my housekeeping is creative rather than

antiseptic.

But this day, I cleaned the refrigerator, dusted, cleaned surfaces, mopped floors, scrubbed kitchen and bathrooms. The house sparkled like a vampire in a cheesy movie. I was tired, sweaty, and filthy with traces of dust, grease, and cleaning products.

"I really like the house when it's clean," PJ commented unwisely when he came home from school and lacrosse practice and flopped onto the sofa to await dinner.

My eyes started to glow red.

"You know where the cleaning products are," I offered sweetly. "And you know about the power switch on the vacuum cleaner."

PJ turned pale, rose slowly and carefully from the couch and backed away from me. The saccharin in my voice hadn't fooled him.

He must have seen the red flicker in my eyes.

Dust Bunny Nursery

Rex, my husband, likes a clean house. So do I. But getting to a clean house, and keeping it there, is a tedious job. Two days ago Rex decided to help me in my wifely duties of housekeeping. He ran the canister vacuum cleaner. It didn't have a bag in it. The dust bunnies apparently mated inside the vacuum cleaner and instantly produced a slew of little dust bunnies that spewed out the back of the cleaner and took over the living room.

It's my fault because we ran out of vacuum cleaner bags. And the local store doesn't carry them for this cleaner model. I had tried to order them on the internet, but when I finally found them I had to deliver a credit card number to a third world country that uses a different alphabet and pay double the cost of the bags in postage and handling. So I decided to check another local store.

They're on backorder.

The new baby dust bunnies grow fast.

I told Rex if he'd wanted a housekeeper he shouldn't have married a courtesan. And if he'd wanted a courtesan, he shouldn't have gotten me pregnant repeatedly. So now he's out of luck.

And I have got to find those vacuum cleaner bags.

Recycling is a Virtue

If I were in a twelve-step program, I'd stand in front of my friendly and concerned fellow-sinners and state "My house is not very well organized" and admit that I need help. So when one of those new stores specializing in organizational equipment moved into the mall and sent out catalogs to the local community, I decided the time had come for me to take charge of my stuff. And Rex's stuff, and Bing's stuff, and PJ's stuff...

The catalog was big. I found clever stacked baskets to sort mail for each family member. Not too expensive, and they looked sleek and efficient. I ordered them. There was a magazine rack for those subscriptions and catalogs that I wanted to keep. Very retro and very chic. One for the living room and one for the den. Plastic bins for toys, unsorted photos, old magazines (Rex has a collection of ski magazines dating to the 1970's), out of season clothes and bits of outdated electronics. I ordered a dozen, assorted sizes.

When my order arrived (how efficient of me to order on the internet and not waste gas!), I plunged into the boxes, scattering foam pellets everywhere in my excitement. In each box, there was a flyer advertising specialty items. Sometimes two flyers.

Surrounded by foam "peanuts", bubble wrap, and plastic bins, I opened a flyer. This month's specials were all to make recycling easier. There were assorted plastic bins for composting vegetable scraps outside, bins for storing compost-to-be in the garage, and decorative – and utilitarian! – containers for storing vegetable peelings and scraps in the kitchen until one is ready to move them into the bin in the garage and, eventually, into the bin in the yard.

They were all made of plastic and looked very sleek and efficient in the flyer. I thought of the empty milk cartons I use to hold cucumber ends and potato peelings. And of the grocery bags that collect recyclable plastics in my kitchen. And I looked at all the purchased plastic, foam "peanuts" and bubble wrap surrounding me and laughed and laughed. Tears ran down my face from laughing so hard. I was glad no one else was home to see me.

I recycled the flyers. And the foam "peanuts." And the cardboard shipping boxes.

Today, the sleek and efficient clever stacked baskets to hold sorted mail for each family member sit on the kitchen counter, overflowing and mostly ignored.

I never bought any more plastic bins, and vegetable scraps for composting still go in empty milk containers until I take them to the outside compost heap, which is back in the bushes and marked off with rusting chicken wire.

Mama Bear sez: It probably isn't a lack of plastic storage devices that is keeping you disorganized. And, don't use more plastic to organize your recycling than you're recycling.

The Inevitable Roaming Laundry Basket

I sat in the dentist's office the other day waiting for a root canal and picked up a copy of one of the magazines that showcase homes that you'll never have, where the decorative clutter is artfully placed and the owner doesn't have to do the dusting. This one featured an ultra-modern condominium in an ultra-big city. Yards of grey granite countertop stretched around the kitchen. There was nothing on top of it. Nothing! No stack of bills, no unread catalogs, no dirty cups (I wasn't really expecting any of those) – not even modernistic stainless steel flour canisters or a glass cylinder holding a single white tulip (I WAS expecting these). The refrigerator had NO MAGNETS ON IT!

The last time Rex and I went refrigerator shopping, we brought along a magnet to test the surfaces to make sure our purchase could also serve as the family memo board. And to collect the souvenir magnets our children pick up for us (we must like magnets, because we have so many, so we get even more of them as gifts – it's a vicious cycle).

This dream habitat included a living room – make that a living space – containing only furniture in shades of pale cream and grey with dusty blue accents and carefully chosen wall art that matched all the furnishings. No gifts from the in-laws, no antique hand-me-downs from grandparents, definitely no artwork from elementary school. I thought of the piles of unsorted mail adorning my plastic kitchen counters and the Betty Boop mantel clock given to me by a dear friend (that now sits shelved in my living room next to the fancy-rock-collection-in-a-Mason-jar that Bing started for me when I told him that a diamond is a fancy rock). I have the homely chachkas that the boys – PJ, Bing, and even my husband Rex – have given me over time. They're lined up in what I hope is an artful manner, sure to set off the wandering laundry basket that occasionally makes its way out of my bedroom. This laundry basket contains the hope of every homemaker, the unmatched socks collected over a span of, in my case, years. I have socks in there (in the lower strata) that are too small to fit anyone in our house.

There's no laundry basket at all in the dream condominium in Chicago. I tried not to drool on the magazine – I hadn't gotten any Novacaine yet, but I guess the other patients waiting in the dentist's office would have just chalked up my drooling to that.

My friends DK (the one who'd given me the Betty Boop clock) and the Blonde Queen (who'd given me the dancing diva doll for my minivan's dashboard) came over after my root canal, bearing assorted tea bags, rice pudding, and sympathy. They asked what they could do for me. I looked at the shelf in the living room with the Betty Boop clock. I looked at the laundry basket sitting off to the side.

"Sort socks," I told them. And they did. I love them.

Of course, the lower strata of small socks remains, slightly disturbed but still intact.

Mama Bear sez: Don't forget that people who have their homes featured in magazines prepare for the photographer to come. They don't really live that way all the time. Ask a plumber or an electrician. (My plumber talked.)

Bunny Butt Decor

I often get knick-knacks as gifts. Sometimes a well-meaning relative will pretend that the item is useful ("It holds soap!" "It decoratively covers a roll of toilet paper!").

Remember, I have a husband and two sons. Knick-knacks are an endangered species at our house ever since the boys learned how to move on their own. Toilet paper roll covers are just camouflage to Rex and the kids, who get confused and think I'm withholding toilet paper. Also, Rex doesn't understand the finer points of home decorating and nobody, including me, understands – or cares to – the finer points of keeping decorative items dusted. So our home decorating consists mostly of displaying the kids' artwork until it falls apart.

One time when some of Rex's family visited, I got a ceramic bunny rabbit with a pump as a hostess gift ("It's useful! It holds soap!"). After the visit, I tucked it under the sink. Yesterday, while rummaging for a dishwasher detergent sample I remembered stashing away, I found the bunny.

Ah, too cute. Its little ceramic furry face rested on its little ceramic furry paws while its little blue ceramic eyes gazed playfully up at me. Its furry little ceramic butt stuck up in the air. It was in the classic "playful puppy" pose (Do rabbits even DO that?). A ceramic garland of blue and pink flowers circled its neck, sweetly entwined with pink ribbons. Its floppy little ceramic ears hung down by its adorable little ceramic face.

I got four cavities just looking at that sweet little thing. Then, on an impulse, I turned it around.

There was a cute little ceramic bunny tail, stuck onto a ceramic bunny butt with a lotion/soap pump sticking out of the top.

The rabbit was mooning the world. I laughed. Rex and the boys laughed, but more at me for laughing so hard.

The cute little ceramic bunny rabbit is now on the kitchen counter, by the sink. I haven't bothered putting soap or hand lotion into this knick-knack. Its usefulness is exclusively decorative. Its cute little bunny face peers out the window while its cute little bunny bottom moons my kitchen.

And I still laugh every time I see it. Now THAT'S decorating!

My New Study

Bing got a job several hours away, working in Our Nation's Capital for a defense contractor. He visits and moans about my new study. It used to be his bedroom, but I transformed it with paint, new carpet, and furniture scrounged from various corners of the earth (like our basement).

I don't know WHY he's complaining, I just know he IS complaining. He took all the furniture out when he moved, so it had to turn into something other than A Shrine to Bing. The only things he left behind were boxes from old electronics ("Don't throw these out! What if I need to return the camera/printer/laser beam particle neutralizer?") and some ancient comic book figurines ("They're collectibles! Someday they'll be valuable! Maybe."). So he has some assorted junk cluttering up our closets, but not enough to justify cluttering up an entire room.

When he visits, he automatically turns into my study, calling it his old room, and expresses wonder that it has been aesthetically transformed. I remind him that I had often offered to purchase paint and equipment so that HE could cover the vintage smudges and spots, but, unless that equipment included robotics capable of wielding a brush, he wasn't interested. He ignores my reminders.

Just to mess with him, sometimes when he visits, I push a portable bed into MY STUDY and let him sleep there, particularly when we have various guests visiting for a major holiday. I could put him in a room with his brother.

But Bing kept me awake a lot when he was a toddler...revenge is, indeed, sweet!

PETS AND OTHER LIFE FORMS

An Ex-Husband is Like a Coach Bag

Rex is older than I am. Not by much, only by 6 weeks or so, but I refer to him as "an older man" because it's technically correct. Sometimes I refer to him as "my first husband" or "my current husband" because those monikers are technically correct, too. He is not really amused by any of this nonsense.

But I am.

Yet, in a way, I feel left out. I have ONE current husband and ONE first husband and they are ONE and the SAME. A lot of my girlfriends have an ex-husband to complain about. I want an ex-husband the way some women want a Coach bag or a pair of Manolo Blahnik pumps. I just want one, but I also want to keep Rex (he's been around, he's fully trained, and he apparently doesn't notice that

I've gained some weight).

One day during a serious discussion with a fairly new girlfriend, I found out that she had not one, not two, but THREE ex-husbands. This is just greedy. She offered me one of hers. We couldn't figure out how to effect the transfer. The discussion got more and more serious, because we were having wine with dinner. We finally decided to postpone further speculations on the legal aspects of this proposed transfer.

Two days later, said girlfriend and I were involved in a volunteer project that brought a retired sports figure into town. He was ensconced in a comfortable and homey inn, at his request, instead of a hotel with round-the-clock service. Unfortunately, said sports figure put the old-fashioned metal key in his room door lock after a late dinner and ripped the top off the key like it was a croissant. Apparently, sports figures – even retired ones – don't always know their own strength. And comfortable and unique inns don't always have concierges – or anyone – available to handle all possible situations. In the ensuing excitement, I found myself in possession of said sports figure's credit card, tracking down a locksmith who'd work late night emergencies, while someone else consoled him and coached him into rehearsing the speech he was planning to deliver in the (rapidly approaching) morning. The locksmith happily referred to me as "Mrs. Sports Figure" (because who else would carry around his credit card and be involved in handling his inconvenient chores?).

Thrice-divorced girlfriend crowed that I finally had my coveted ex-husband.

"What do you mean?" I asked.

"You're Mrs. Sports Figure!" she explained.

"Ah," I said. "When is the divorce final?"

"When the lock is fixed and the locksmith goes away."

"Wouldn't it be when I give back the credit card?" I wanted to know.

"You're Mrs. Sports Figure. You KEEP the credit card when you get divorced." She is a knowledgeable woman, and experienced, too.

Of course, I gave the credit card back. This way I can complain about how cheap my ex-husband is.

Mama Bear sez: You CAN get what you want, or at least sort of. If you have enough imagination, or at least a friend with enough imagination.

Rex, Unsatisfied

In the early, halcyon days of my marriage to Rex – pre-children, when I thought things were romantic and all the world existed with gauzy lighting and pastels (like our wedding photos) – we often went away with friends for weekends, or went on evening picnics at beach houses owned by the parents of our friends and populated with other young couples.

One such soft summer evening, mere months into our marriage, we sat around a cheerful fire, drinking inexpensive wine from paper cups and admiring a sunset across a misty New England lake, a view paid for by the grandparents of Rex's ex-roommate. Always eager to practice his hosting skills, said roommate pecked away at the relaxed mood with a series of questions that sounded like they'd come from a book called "Fun Parlor Games to Amuse Your Friends Unless They Are Watching a Lovely Sunset in the Arms of Their Beloved, In Which Case They Will Probably Be More Annoyed Than Amused."

But I felt magnanimous – after all, the view WAS courtesy of his grandparents, and Rex and I were deeply in love and newly married. Annoying ex-roommate then turned to Rex and me.

"What is your favorite song?" he asked me.

I relaxed into Rex's arms and smiled dreamily. Sighing, I named the overly romantic song I'd selected for our first dance at our wedding reception. I smiled up into Rex's face.

"And yours?" Annoying ex-roommate turned to Rex after dutifully noting my answer in a notebook he was inexplicably using to record this nonsense.

Rex frowned thoughtfully. His face cleared and he beamed at his friend.

"'I Can't Get No Satisfaction' by the Rolling Stones!" he offered, with enthusiasm.

A brief silence, then uproarious, cheap-wine fueled laughter shattered the romantic mood. Rex didn't understand until his ex-roommate helpfully, and thoroughly, explained.

There wasn't a shred of the romantic mood left.

Merry Christmas!
Love, Santa

My family's Christmas traditions aren't found in women's magazines. One of my cousins makes gingerbread men and decorates them to represent famous people or the relatives. One year she gave my younger brother a cookie of a young Hungarian gymnast who was in the Olympics. This cousin is masterful, and the gymnast was recognizable. She gave my mother a cookie of a blue-eyed movie star, naked but for a strategically placed icing fig leaf. My mother, never one to be outdone in the Christmas tradition department, annually tucks a present for my father under the tree, labeled to show it's from a sultry Italian actress.

I decided to continue these traditions. I make gingerbread men – and women and children – and decorate them somewhat less imaginatively than my cousin, but they are popular.

And I leave imaginative presents from Santa for Rex and the boys.

The year Rex was 49, Santa left him a special present. I had found an exquisite item on a sale rack. It was a lumpy ball, the size of a child's fist, sporting dozens of inch-long tentacles. The entire...object...was thickly covered with gold glitter, even the tentacles. It had a loop attached, and hung with unwanted Christmas ornaments on a neglected little rack in the back of a department store. I found the rack by accident. It was marked down. Way down. I thought it would be a joke for a girlfriend (the Beehived Singer Girlfriend) who adorns gift packages with glitter and glitz.

But then inspiration hit me. With a two-by-four. Hard. Santa gave the present to Rex in honor of his looming 50th birthday. Santa included a gift tag informing Rex that this ornament was to remind him that this upcoming year he'd be eligible for his first colonoscopy.

I laughed in an undignified fashion. So did my mother. Rex was not nearly as amused as I was. Neither was my father.

Too bad.

My mother hung the ornament from the brass chandelier over our dining table (it's no secret where I get THAT sense of humor). At every meal for a month I stifled giggles while Rex eyed me censoriously.

I can't believe I got that fabulously entertaining item for 90% off!

Mama Bear sez: Amuse yourself whenever you can. And blame Santa.

The Dog I Didn't Get

My life hasn't been all roses and California alcoholic products. I once wanted a dog, really, really badly, and Rex nixed the idea.

As newlyweds, Rex and I lived in one of those fashionably "transitioning" inner city neighborhoods, where newly renovated and "it'll be a good investment" apartment buildings are tucked amid crack houses. Eventually, brave developers buy and restore enough crack houses to tip the balance and the neighborhood becomes truly upscale – and all the drug dealers relocate to a neighborhood across town where the pricey apartment houses are lapsing into genteel seediness and, eventually, become tomorrow's drug dens.

I'd been mugged in front of our renovated crack house-turned-nice-apartment. In broad daylight, by a teenager who looked like he'd just come from choir practice at the local cathedral, dressed in a collared shirt and neat khaki slacks. I'd hit the ground hollering, and about a dozen ex-Marines and gym enthusiasts swarmed out of the building. My assailant dropped everything (except an ID card so he'd be easy to find) and ran. He had a head start, and escaped. An emergency room visit and six stitches later, I wanted a dog.

We'd already planned on buying a house and moving to the suburbs, and the owner of a sturdy three-bedroom Colonial had accepted our offer. I was petrified. I wouldn't have a building full of ex-Marines and muscled gym rats to answer my howls. I'd be isolated by a yard and decorative plantings. I wanted a dog.

I told everyone I met that I wanted a dog. It didn't matter to me that Rex emphatically did not want one.

My prayers were answered. A distant

acquaintance with professional dog training experience had seen a mid-sized German shepherd pushed out of a car at the park where he and his son were playing. He had five dogs, which his wife insisted was his limit, but he prepared this beauty to be placed. She had basic training, shots and a thorough vet check. She was spayed and just entering adulthood. All her rescuer wanted was a good home for her. Enter me.

Rex said no. He had reasons, like we were never home on weekends, and we were away at work all day, every weekday. But these paled, in my mind, to the terror I felt being alone, in the suburbs, with a house that creaked and branches that sighed in the wind, and fresh mugging scars on my head and my psyche.

We didn't get the dog.

By now, she'd be long dead. But Rex will hear this story for the rest of our marriage.

He's been hearing this story already for a lot of years...

By the way, the scars both inside and outside my head have healed. And, to be truthful, we're still not home much, and I wouldn't want to have to take care of a dog. But don't tell Rex.

It Must Be The Y Chromosome

Bing moved a couple of hundred miles from us, lives in an apartment and works in information technology, which I think means he talks to computers all day. When he visits, he introduces me to all sorts of internet web sites. I've learned how to check a web site for proper security before I purchase anything, how to find out where a web site originates, who will sell me odd services like writing a limerick or editing a photo, and just how very much incorrect information can be found, on any topic imaginable.

I introduce him to parts of my life, too, even though sometimes he tries to stop me. On a recent visit, Bing insisted that my story about the horse at the nearby barn with a fetish for the owner's mad bomber hat is disturbing. A gorgeous but mature gentleman horse became infatuated with the brown plaid and fake rabbit fur hat his owner dons when the weather is below freezing. He nickers suggestively when she's wearing it, and tries to follow her.

She insists that she only wears the hat because it keeps her warm and, if she's wearing it, she doesn't have to look at it. The horse likes to look at it. So everyone is fairly happy.

Except Bing. He is quite unhappy with this information, and says I have too much imagination. I say the elderly horse is the one with too much imagination. Bing changes the subject by showing me cartoons from the internet. I find many of them disturbing, on many levels.

Bing has a double standard. He obviously thinks moms can be too disgusting really easily, but it is impossible for sons to be too disgusting.

If I complain about this, Rex suggests Bing

wasn't raised properly. So now when I complain, I add that it must be caused by Y chromosomes.

I like to get the last word. Rex says THAT'S from having too many X chromosomes.

Alien Encounters

There are aliens in our house. Regularly. And before getting too excited, everyone should take a deep breath and look up "alien" in the dictionary: "1....foreign. 2. strange...noun...3. an outsider..." (from Webster's New World Dictionary, Third College Edition).

We have cats, as well as teenagers. And if we really look into it, males and females are alien to each other (see the definition that includes "strange").

Our most recent feline acquisition, Boo (also known as "Dr. Evil" for his tendency to try to discipline humans with mild nips and claws), habitually chases his tail, catches it, subdues it with vigorous bites, screeches in pain and releases it. This is alien. My children are astounded by the strangeness. I am, too, although I frequently pet him. I like him.

Boo, at 10 months, already had a past checkered with crimes and incarceration. He had been in the animal shelter for several weeks under the guise of being checked for rabies because he bit someone, while the tender-hearted animal control officer, May, hunted for a suitable home for him. And conned the Chief of Police, an avowed cat hater who remains suspicious of all felines kept at town expense, with the story that rabies, or some other horrible disease, could show up any minute and then he'd be allowed to slay the cat. May offered me Boo when I came to pick up the corpse of our orange and white tabby, MK Ultra, who'd lost her fight with an SUV. I was sad about MK Ultra, but reasoned that a short happy life of keeping the neighborhood free of rampaging polar bears and rogue elephants was preferable to a longer but more sedate indoor existence to MK's half-feral heart. May liked that. Or maybe she figured any home for Boo was better than none; he was running out of time at the animal shelter. She palmed Boo off on me, warning me that he bites and nobody wants him. I assured her that I outweighed Boo by enough to not be too worried about his bad habits.

I'm a sucker. And being willing to take on a recognized biter was an alien concept to much of my family...

And so this alien joined our family.

One of my goddaughters, the one who looks like a Da Vinci Madonna, stays overnight once a week for convenience (hers, mine and her parents'). Boo took one look at her and claimed her. She walks in the door, and he saunters over to her. He's casual, a teenager with a crush playing it cool. Then he tails her for her entire visit. If Da Vinci Madonna Goddaughter leaves the room, Boo follows her at a distance, indifferent, seemingly even unaware that he's doing this. But he never loses track of his favorite person.

Boo even taught her to hunt, with infinite patience. We have decorative magnets on our refrigerator which hold up soccer schedules, notices of furnace cleanings and oil changes due, and cartoons criticizing meals made with tofu (thank you, Son Number One). Two of these magnets are needlepoint dinosaurs in improbable colors. Boo likes to pull these magnets off the refrigerator; he can dig his claws into them.

One evening I walked into the kitchen and Da Vinci Madonna Goddaughter was sitting attentively and gracefully on the floor while Boo pulled down the red dinosaur magnet with one paw, gave it a quick bite (apparently to finalize the kill) and then stretched his paw out to her, offering her the prey. She carefully thanked him, took the magnet and replaced it on the refrigerator door. This went on for twenty minutes, each of them fully absorbed.

In the evening, Boo demands to be let into the guest room where his Da Vinci Madonna Goddess sleeps. Once in, he walks the perimeter, checking windows, under the bed, desk and dresser, and behind the closet door. Then he settles in, at the doorway, and guards her all night.

She seems grateful, thanks him, and seems to understand him.

Maybe I'm the alien here.

156

Delightful Dentistry

My dentist likes me. I've been going to him for a long time. A very long time. Since before I met my husband. He's given me a lot of fillings. And caps. And things. I've given him a lot of money.

The last time I saw him, he was replacing an old cap on one of my molars. He and his assistant complimented me. I was on my back, mouth open, eyes closed (who wants to see close-ups of scary tools?) and fists clenched (at least I don't whimper, like I used to).

The compliment? (They both assured me that it IS a compliment...) They told me that I'm so quiet and still that working on me is like working on a dead person.

I don't want to know how they know that. I do want to know how comparing me to a corpse qualifies as a compliment.

And he has sincerely discussed with me (one-sidedly, he had his hands and three tools in my mouth) his bewilderment at why people don't like dentist appointments...

The Fashionista Freedom Fighter

I recently lost weight. Quite a bit of weight (over 70 pounds). On purpose. How and why is another story, but one side effect is that I needed a new wardrobe. And one of the things I wanted was a fitted vintage blazer. I'd wanted one since I was in college, many years ago, but when my wallet was finally fat enough, my waist was too thick. Finally, waist whittled and bank account sufficiently padded, I was in shape for a fine, tailored, vintage jacket.

My Beehive Coiffed Singer Girlfriend (doesn't everyone have one?) recommended a monthly vintage clothing tag sale, where she picks up – and sells – various outfits, including the fabulous 1950's and 1960's outfits she uses for her shows. She suggested I go to Thalia, one of the women who run it, explain my situation and place myself under the protection of her oh-so-competent Fashionista Sense.

So I did. The tag sale is held in an unusually spacious first floor apartment in a newly trendy neighborhood consisting of old brownstones with an occasional Victorian rooming house tucked in between. The neighborhood includes several cutting-edge coffee shops but isn't too fashionable for a wide mix of stores and residents. Walking into the apartment-turned-vintage-sartorial-paradise was like entering an Aladdin's cave of clothes, with a complimentary glass of champagne and all the glitter and glam a newly-svelte could desire.

I got the perfect vintage fitted jacket, complete with elaborate seaming, rhinestone buttons, and a garment tag from a fabulous 5th Avenue shop from the 1950's. I also got some of the best fashion advice I've ever heard. Wish I'd heard it as a teen-ager while I was fretting with what at the time I considered frizzy hair (now it's "Naturally Curly! Yay!"), freckles ("They are so cute!") and thick ankles (there's no way to salvage those – so I simply don't wear shoes with ankle straps...).

Thalia busily provided me with the full gamut of Fashionista Free Advice. I gratefully soaked it up, along with my glass of champagne. Thalia tossed clothes to me, periodically patting some part of my anatomy to check for size (How initially startling! Score one for the champagne as a natural relaxant), stepping back to assess the fit of a clothing item, or screwing up her face in concentration before delivering The Verdict ("The sleeves are 1/2 inch too short. You'll never really like it" or "You really look best in tailored items" or "This is perfect on you. Perfect. Look at Carol, everyone. How perfect is that dress/skirt/vest? Step back. Here's a mirror. Look at you! Just look at you!").

I'd amassed a stack of lovely items, each of which Thalia deemed suitable and I'd decided I liked. Thalia never tried to override my decision if I didn't like a color or thought I'd never wear an item. She'd just shrug and move on, a whirlwind of advice and admiration.

One pair of delicious slacks slipped into my hands from the tireless Thalia. The fabric felt like thick silk, the color a deep midnight blue. I wanted them without even trying them on. These slacks would take me to the Wide World of Ultra-Glam, frizzy hair be damned!

"Slacks are hard to fit," warned Thalia as I ducked behind the screen that acted as one of the fitting rooms. I did not pay any attention. I was too busy trying not to drool on the fabric.

The slacks did not fit me. They stretched tight over my upper hips and bunched in the crotch. There was no corrective underwear or simple tailoring that would fix the problem. I moaned softly and caressed the fabric as I handed them back to Thalia.

"My butt is still too fat," I apologized.

The flurry of activity stopped. Immediately.
Heads turned to stare at me as all the women in
the room stilled. Thalia stared at me in horror,
frozen, lips parted.

The moment stretched. Finally, Thalia shook it
off. The others still watched, horrified.

"No," Thalia stated firmly. "There is NOTHING
wrong with you or with your butt. The slacks
are wrong. Clothes have a job to do. Their job
is to make YOU look fabulous. If they do not do
that, they fail and we reject them." With that,
Thalia flung the offending slacks across the
room, where they collapsed into a little heap of
failure. Everyone else turned away, and I
stared, my turn to be frozen in shock, into
Thalia's wise face.

She is a Fashionista Freedom Fighter.

I love her, and women across the country who have heard her wisdom love her, too. She's our new hero.

Mama Bear sez: Listen to Thalia: clothes work for you and if they don't fit, they are not doing their job. Fire them.

Confessions of an Out of Date Techno-Geek

Once upon a time, I met Bill Gates of Microsoft fame. I worked for him. Not directly, but eventually the chain of command stretched all the way to his office. I was a part-time representative for Microsoft, working from my home but technically based out of a large city nearby. Two large companies in the small city 10 miles away depended on me to convince them that Microsoft products were the best for their needs.

At an annual convention for the support staff of which I was a member, I won a beach towel which I still have and got an autograph on a paper napkin from Mr. Gates, which I framed and gave away to an admirer (Mr. Gates's admirer, not mine) at one of the aforementioned large companies.

So I used to be technologically astute. (I wasn't fired from Microsoft for lacking computer savvy, I gave birth to PJ and left for other pastures—another long story...) Anyway, now I'm no longer even technologically adequate.

Last week, I learned how to use the zoom on our new digital camera. After trumpeting my discovery to Rex and the boys (now teens), I expected praise and humble requests to teach them the secret. But they already knew how to zoom in on the subject.

I soothed my wounded pride by noting that I'm the only one who actually read the manual.

Further Confessions of an Out of Date Techno-Geek

Before PJ, before Bing and even before Rex, I worked for a giant computer company that sold and serviced giant computers. Now, Bing helps me turn off the double-click function on my laptop. I don't even remember what a double-click function IS from one week to the next, and don't really care unless I accidentally turn it on and re-booting the computer doesn't turn it back off.

Bing is a computer geek. He told me the other day that my laptop can write DVDs. I put a round silver disk in the DVD player/writer and tried to copy a video file. It didn't work. He told me it was a CD, not a DVD. But they look the same. He tried to explain the difference. I pretended to understand it, and nodded a lot. I didn't have a clue what he was explaining. Bing tends to look at me suspiciously when I nod a lot and sometimes accuses me of being lost, and sometimes I even admit up to it. This time he just sighed.

If I'm home alone and want to watch a movie, I randomly select one of the four remotes decorating our coffee table and keep pressing buttons, discarding remotes and picking up others until something happens. Sometimes I end up watching television instead of a movie. Sometimes I listen to the radio. Sometimes I go to bed early and read a book after throwing the remotes against the wall. I've been doing a lot of reading since the fourth remote entered the house.

I'm not totally hopeless, though. I HAVE mastered how to throw away tops off of ANY food packaging – from beer bottle caps to foil yogurt tops. I find it easy to move any of these or similar items the two feet between most counter surfaces in our convenient kitchen and the trash receptacle. Rex can't do that, and

Bing and PJ seem to have inherited that gene from him. I think as a reward for my accomplishment, I'm going to set up a separate television in the guest room that only I use. It'll be always ready, at the push of one single solitary button, which I will have well marked in neon pink, to play a DVD. Or a CD.

Whatever.

Attempted Intervention

I shared some of these stories with friends, and with Rex, Bing and PJ. Hours after Bing, visiting for the holidays, read my versions of his youthful experiences, he approached me. Actually, he cornered me in the kitchen while I was rinsing beans for soup. He was always the problem solver, and, apparently, he'd been chosen by his father and brother to handle this delicate situation.

"Mom, you need a hobby." Not exactly a subtle beginning.

"I have one, Son Number One – being a mom to you and your brother." I smiled sweetly and dumped the rinsed and sorted beans into a big pot. I wasn't going down easily on this one.

"We're getting older, and moving on with our lives. What do you like to do outside of..." Bing

171

paused. I know my child. I could see him struggle to find something to say other than "tormenting us." Bing took a hasty breath and plunged in. "Other than writing stories about us."

"I do like to amuse people with stories," I admitted, and reached for an onion. I quickly planned my strategy, and the onion was key.

"Well, Mom, these stories of yours are the literary equivalent of showing embarrassing baby photos. To everyone. And, frankly, Dad and PJ think you may exaggerate a little bit." I pulled a paring knife from the knife block on the counter. I'd selected the dull one. Strategy.

"I'm shocked! My stories are fiction!" I looked up at Bing with wide, sincere eyes while I placed the onion on the cutting board and halved it with the not-quite-sharp blade. The bruised bulb sent irritating fumes billowing into my face.

"Sure, Mom. Look, PJ's afraid that he'll never keep a girlfriend because of these stories."

"I see," I said, my eyes beginning to water under attack from the onion vapor.

"Dad's embarrassed."

"How unfortunate," I added, and two tears slid down my checks.

"Would you like to take an adult education course in...maybe...painting? Or restoring old cars?" Bing's resolve weakened.

"No," I stated firmly, hacking at the onion and blinking furiously to clear my vision. I didn't want to lose a finger.

"You like my Del Sol, and it needs a little restoration from where you hit it."

"I didn't hit it very hard," I protested, tears now rolling down my face. Luckily, Bing didn't attempt a consoling hug. He might have noticed the onion fumes and connected them to my ready tears. I think he held back because of the enthusiastic way I was brandishing the knife.

"Maybe tennis? Or graphic art? Or baseball, or stock trading?" Bing appeared ready to bolt.

"I'll think about it," I assured him, wiping my face with my sleeve. "I'm sorry, I may need a moment here," I apologized. Bing fled, and I heard no more.

Two days later, for Christmas, I received an interesting, and very generous, array of gifts: a book on decoupage and supplies to make a decorative box, a set of calligraphy pens (I guess they figured if I insisted upon writing, they'd at least slow me down), a new tennis racket and a can of balls, a book on Tai Chi and a gift certificate for four horseback riding lessons. Rex, Bing and PJ all looked very hopeful as I exclaimed over each present.

Maybe I'll take up horseback riding...

EPILOGUE: IT'S NEVER THE END

Dear Readers,

An "epilogue" is defined in Webster's dictionary as "the closing section of a novel, or a play." There is no end to the Domestic Underground. Wherever toilets explode, and students ask their parents homework questions until they graduate, and parents face challenges with humor, the Domestic Underground survives. This is, however, the end of this particular collection from the front lines of Motherhood. But life with Mama Bear continues, sometimes with borrowed children – and grandchildren – to remind her that revolving doors and department store escalators make grand adventures...and, sometimes with horseback riding, to teach her that there exist some large hairy critters that can be told what to do, and will do it!

Thank you for sharing these adventures!

Carol

~~~

Hello, Carol,

It is a Tuesday in somewhat sunny, reasonably cold, Northern State Full of Mountains.

I have a list of "must do's", well maybe only "I've put them off as long as I can do's". But I do have a list:

1) (blah-blah)
2) (more blah-blah)
3) (blah-blah-blah)
4) (yada yada)
a) (sub-yada)
b) (more sub-yada)
5) Begin and FINISH writing the 25 odd descriptions of the art for the next exhibit here

6) Contact my art promoter in LA about the CW exhibit and his request for my WPA art for Joplin, MO

7) Contact the Wethersfield art teacher with whom I am working on a mural project

8) Write some letters that should have been sent at Christmas

9) Read Notes from the Domestic Underground

I decided in my infinite wisdom to read Notes from the Domestic Underground.

I started from the beginning and stumbled over "Beep Beep". Or I should say – I stumbled, fell, was dazed, got up bloody and bruised and with an entirely different outlook on life. My life is split asunder and I must re-frame my future.

I have often wondered why after talking with me people run to the shoe store to purchase hip boots. Perhaps I should write on my forehead "Caution: Hip Boots Required".

Perhaps I should rename my planned book Beep Beep with my Burro instead of Tales with my Burro....

No offense taken of course. Thank you for my education,

John Stewart
Director, Amity Art Foundation

(You're welcome, John. I'm glad you now understand why I beep at you sometimes!
- Carol)

~~~

Dear Fellow Readers,

"Mama Bear", who, in addition to being one of my most favorite people in the world, is one of the smartest, wittiest and most spirited women I have ever met (just a few of the many reasons she is a favorite!).

Reading Notes from The Domestic Underground, I laughed, I cried, and reminisced about reading Erma Bombeck's, The Grass is Always Greener Over the Septic Tank.

I am reminded once again to not take life too seriously, one can find humor in just about anything and our women friends mean so very much that it almost can't be put into words.

I cannot wait for volume 2, in hopes of seeing the stories about 'names for cysts' and the threat she made to "PJ" when he was well into his teens!

(I think I'm) The Mother of Angel Face and The Princess

(Thank you, my friend. Maybe you are The Princess and Angel Face's mother, but only if you're flattered - Carol)

~~~

(And, finally, one last comment...)

To Whom it May Concern:

I am not Rex.

Sincerely,
Carol's husband